For my own pajamakkah lovers, DH, EL, ET, EV, and my Elterman family.
—DH

For all kids who celebrate this beautiful holiday!
— O&A Ivanovs

Text © 2024 by Dara Henry
Illustrations by Olga & Aleksey Ivanov
Cover and internal design © 2024 by Sourcebooks

Sourcebooks and the colophon are registered trademarks of Sourcebooks.

The full color art was created digitally in a pencil and watercolor style.

Published by Sourcebooks Jabberwocky, an imprint of Sourcebooks Kids
P.O. Box 4410, Naperville, Illinois 60567-4410
(630) 961-3900
sourcebookskids.com

Cataloging-in-Publication Data is on file with the Library of Congress.

Source of Production: Wing King Tong Paper Products Co. Ltd., Shenzhen, Guangdong Province, China
Date of Production: February 2024
Run Number: 5037511

Printed and bound in China.
WKT 10 9 8 7 6 5 4 3 2 1

# Hanukkah Pajamakkahs

Words by Dara Henry
Pictures by Olga & Aleksey Ivanov

sourcebooks
jabberwocky

It was the first night of Hanukkah and Ruthie couldn't wait to celebrate.
She tore open her Hanukkah present and squealed in delight.

"pajamakkahs!"

"You can wear them to the Hanukkah Pajamakkah Party!" Ruthie's dad said, ruffling her hair.

"But I wanna wear my Hanukkah pajamakkahs *all* eight nights!"

"Well, okay..." Ruthie's mom said, "just make sure you keep them spotless for the party."

"I'll be very careful," Ruthie promised as she headed to the kitchen. Her little sister Sarah raced ahead. "Let's make latkes!"

Ruthie grated onions and potatoes, sprinkled salt, and even flipped and fried.

Golden latkes sizzled in the pan. Ruthie taste-tested bite after bite.

"Those are just streaks," Ruthie said, with a wipe.
"My Hanukkah pajamakkahs are still *spot*less."

On the second night, when it came time to recite the prayers, Ruthie took safety measures.

She held the shamash and lit the first candle.

"Just a splotch!" Ruthie said. "My Hanukkah pajamakkahs are still *spot*less."

On the third night, Ruthie wrapped gifts and hired a guard dog.
"Patches will protect my pajamakkahs."
But an unexpected game of chase turned into trouble.

CRINKLE!

"That's definitely not a spot," said Ruthie, scratching at the strips of tape.

On the fourth night, Ruthie's family stopped by her cousin Jake's house for sufganiyot and soccer.

Staying spotless would be easy.

But the hoodie made it hard to see.

Dad groaned. "Glitter never comes off!"
Ruthie grinned. "Sparkly, not spotty!"

But when she leaped before looking, Ruthie ended up covered...

SQUISH!

"Ooey, gooey!" she licked her fingers. "But my Hanukkah pajamakkahs are still *spot*less."

On the fifth night of Hanukkah, Ruthie
had another idea. She and Sarah crafted
holiday place mats. "I've got this covered!"

On the sixth night of Hanukkah, Ruthie got gimmels and chocolate gelt and twirled like a top.

"My Hanukkah pajamakkahs are still spot-free!"

As Ruthie got ready for bed, she saw streaks and splotches, sparkles and squishes, but no spots. If the oil could last eight nights, so could her Hanukkah pajamakkahs!

But night seven didn't go exactly as planned. The holiday sing-along got sloppy, and the make-your-own menorahs were a mistake.

SPLISH!

"No spots here!"

On the last night of Hanukkah, everyone got dressed for the family pajamakkah party.

Mom and Dad looked at Ruthie's pajamakkahs.
"Oh my!" Mom said.

"It's a miracle those pajamakkahs made it through *all* eight nights,"
Dad chuckled. "But I see spots."
"Dotted, not spotted." Ruthie smiled.

Family trickled in. Everyone listened to music, ate latkes, and played games.

Then it was time for the family pajamakkah photo!

"One last spin," said Ruthie...

There were spills and splatters, plops and globs, smudges and smears and sparkles and...

"My Hanukkah pajamakkahs are finally spotted!"
Ruthie laughed. "It really *is* a Hanukkah miracle."